"Maybe. But probably not. Tonight would be a hard act to follow. Sleep tight, now."

Leila tucks her face in her covers, cozy as a bat wrapped up in her wings. Even with her eyes closed, she can still see the black shapes. She watches them wheel and glide, wheel and glide, until, breath by breath, she feels herself lifting and spinning: an acrobat tumbling across the dark sky.

"We saw ducks, a star, and a skunk. And too many bats to count," she hears Daddy tell Mama.

Leila squints at the window, but the outside has disappeared. The dark glass is a mirror reflecting them in the bright room. Daddy bends down, and Mama kisses Leila.

"Sweet dreams, Bat Watcher," says Mama.

"Maybe tomorrow we'll see even more bats," Leila murmurs as Daddy carries her to bed.

The sliding door skims open, then bangs softly
shut as Daddy carries Leila inside. The light
makes her cover her face.

Two bats flutter and turn in midair, looping and crossing. Another swings past like a black boomerang, too fast to follow. More waltz and hook, sweeping the sky: hungry bats showing off as they gather their insect feast. Daddy and Leila laugh and clap.

"It's a bat bonanza!" Daddy shouts.

"Aren't they clever?" Leila squirms, straining to catch every stunt. "It's like a circus! Hello, Mr. Bat! Hello, Mrs. Bat! Hello, Mary Ann! Hello!"

At last she sinks back and yawns.

Mosquitoes buzz. It's getting chilly. Leila is almost ready to give up when she spots the first blur of wings.

"Saw one!" She grabs Daddy by the sleeve.

"Remember this? 'Twinkle, twinkle, little bat,'" Daddy sings.

"Shh! That's a silly song," Leila scolds.

"Last night we didn't see any bats," Daddy remembers.

"But the night before that we saw five."

Far away, a car rumbles. Closer, they hear the mumble of someone's TV. Nearer still, almost under them, something crunches through dry leaves.

Daddy carries Leila to the porch rail. Just in time, they watch their visitor's furry white stripes disappear.

"So long, Mr. Skunk," Leila whispers.

In the backyard, the leaves are like black paper cutouts against the darkening sky.

Very quietly, Leila and Daddy call together: "Bats, bats, come, oh bats!"

A line of ducks flaps past a star. Leila snuggles closer to Daddy.

"'Twinkle, twinkle, little star,'" she sings in a very small voice.

"You sang that very nicely," says Daddy.

"Do you think the star liked it?"

"I liked it."

"But I wasn't singing to you. I was singing to the star. Do you think my voice flew all the way up there?"

"A star's a long way away," Daddy tells her.

"I'll bet a bat could fly that far," says Leila.

"I've had my bath. See? I'm wearing my nightgown!"

Daddy yawns. "Then it must be bedtime."

"Not yet!" Leila shrieks. "I'll give you one clue. What rhymes with mat time?"

"Rat time? Gnat time? Hat time?" Daddy guesses as he carries Leila outside.

"'And Goldilocks never went back there again,'" Daddy reads.

Mama looks up from her book. "Guess what time it is."

"Dinner time!" Daddy answers.

"We already ate dinner," Leila reminds him.

"Bath time?"

"Okay, now." Daddy tickles Leila's ear with the tip of her braid. "I think we have time for exactly one story."

Leila gives the sky a last, hard look before she takes his hand. Soon bats will come looking for their food.

A yellow cat slinks down the sidewalk, then stalks white moths on the lawn. Leila claps her hands.

"Psst!" she hisses. "Go away, Coriander! Don't you dig up my mother's flowers!" The cat slouches under a bush, sniffing for mice.

Leila runs to the front door in her nightgown and peers out at the garden. Between the snapdragons and the asters, the flowering tobacco plants have opened into bundles of bright, white stars. Their soft night smell floats through the screen door to Leila.

"Okay, stars." Leila giggles. "Fly into the sky and bring me my bats!"

"If I had a bat of my own," she adds, stepping onto the rug, "I'd call her Mary Ann, and it would always be bat time."

"You'd still have to wait until dark to see her. In the day, she'd cover herself with her wings, like this." Mama wraps the big blue towel around Leila.

"Why would someone be afraid of bats?" Leila asks a little later, when she's in her bath.

Mama thinks for a moment. "Maybe because there's nothing else like them," she says. "They look like mice, and they fly like birds, but they aren't mice or birds."

"That's why they're so special," says Leila. She wrings out her washcloth and pulls the plug from the drain.

Mr. Mackety's hair is so white that it glows against the tree trunks. But the leaves at the tops of the trees still sparkle with sunlight.

Bats don't come out until the first star shines.

Mr. Mackety smiles. "Well, you can keep 'em!
They give me the creeps."

"Hello, Mr. Mackety!" Leila calls to her neighbor. "I'm waiting for bats!"

"Bats!" Mr. Mackety's bicycle squeaks to a stop. "Now, what would a nice little girl like you want with bats? Aren't you scared they'll get caught in your hair?"

"Bats never bump into things. Not even in the dark. They're very good flyers," says Leila.

Daddy hangs the broom on its hook and
pushes the chairs under the table. "Aren't you the
impatient one tonight?"

"Is it bat time now?" Leila asks as she carefully tips the dustpan into the trash.

"Hello, Mr. Perrault! Hello, Ms. Kottmeir!"
she calls.

It's too early for bats.

Outside, shadows stripe the sidewalk. The sun glints through the trees, making Leila squint her eyes.

"All done!" says Leila, licking the sweet berry
juice off her lips and pushing her plate aside. "Can
we look for bats now?"

Daddy wipes Leila's sticky red fingers. "Bats? At
this hour? Go look out the window and then you
tell me."

For David, with love

—R.H.

For Ellie and her dad

—S.A.

Text copyright © 1991 by Ruth Horowitz

Illustrations copyright © 1991 by Susan Avishai

Four Winds Press

Macmillan Publishing Company

866 Third Avenue, New York, NY 10022

Collier Macmillan Canada, Inc.

1200 Eglinton Avenue East, Suite 200

Don Mills, Ontario M3C 3N1

Printed and bound in Hong Kong

First American Edition

10 9 8 7 6 5 4 3 2 1

The text of this book is set in 16 point Jenson.
The illustrations are rendered in water-soluble colored pencil.
Library of Congress Cataloging-in-Publication Data
Horowitz, Ruth. Bat time / Ruth Horowitz ;
illustrated by Susan Avishai. — 1st American ed. p. cm.
Summary: Before she goes to bed, Leila shares a special moment with
her father watching bats enjoying an insect feast in the backyard.
I S B N 0 - 0 2 - 7 4 4 5 4 1 - 0
[1. Bats—Fiction. 2. Fathers and daughters—Fiction.]
I. Avishai, Susan, ill. II. Title.
PZ7.H7877Bat 1991 [E]—dc20 90-35772

BAT TIME

Ruth Horowitz

Illustrated by

Susan Avishai

Four Winds Press   New York
Collier Macmillan Canada   Toronto
Maxwell Macmillan International Publishing Group
New York   Oxford   Singapore   Sydney